Tricked for Treats!

A Rugrats Halloween

KLASKY CSUPO INC.

Based on the TV series *Rugrats*® created by Arlene Klasky, Gabor Csupo, and
Paul Germain as seen on Nickelodeon®

ISBN 0-439-13557-5

12 11 10 9 8 7 6 5 4 3 2 1   9/9 0 1 2 3 4/0

Printed in the U.S.A.   08

First Scholastic printing, October 1999

NICKELODEON®

RUGRATS™

Tricked for Treats!

A Rugrats Halloween

by Sarah Willson
illustrated by Don Cassity

SCHOLASTIC INC.
New York Toronto London Auckland Sydney
Mexico City New Delhi Hong Kong

"Our house is going to be the scariest one on the block this year!" said Tommy's father, Stu. "The place looks great, Deed."

Tommy's mother, Didi, frowned. "The house does look nice, Stu. But all this candy isn't good for children. Look how much the kids got at their Halloween party!"

She pointed to Angelica and the babies, who were holding plastic pumpkins full of treats. "Maybe I should go make some wheat-germ pumpkin muffins to pass out to the trick-or-treaters."

"Why, when I was a boy, there was no such thing as healthy food!" declared Grandpa Lou. "We ate sugar by the box! Now, where did I put my teeth?" He walked upstairs to search for them.

Stu rolled his eyes. "Kids don't want healthy food on Halloween, Deed. The spirit of Halloween is about getting candy!"

"What's the spirit of Halloween?" asked Chuckie.

"Beats me," Tommy replied.

Suddenly Angelica had an idea. She stopped sorting her candy and looked up at the babies. "You mean to tell me that you babies never heard of the spirit of Halloween?" she asked slyly.

"N-n-no," said Chuckie.

Angelica lowered her voice. "There are actually *all kinds* of spirits! There are ghosts and gobblings and grumblins and stuff. They come around every year at this time. They haunt babies until they give up their candy! But if you give *me* your candy, I'll make sure you babies don't get haunted this year!"

"Yes, sir, just give me your candy, and I'll tell the scary ghosts to go away," Angelica continued, stepping behind the couch and quietly opening up a toy box. She wound up some toys and set them on the floor. "Hey, look!" She pointed at the toys that were coming toward the babies.

"What's the matter, Angelica?" said Tommy.

"Don't you see, you dumb babies?" said Angelica. "Those toys are walking all by themselves! The ghosts are already here, haunting you!"

Suddenly eerie music began playing. It was coming from behind the couch.

Chuckie reached into his pumpkin and pulled out a Reptar bar. "H-h-here, Angelica!" he called, holding it out to her. "Give those ghosts a Reptar bar and ask them to please go away!"

Angelica took the candy bar and put it into her pumpkin. "I can't believe how easy it is to take candy from a baby!" she cackled to herself.

"Tommy, we're doomed!" wailed Chuckie. "The spirits of Halloween are right here in your house, right there behind your couch! And they want our candy!"

"Wait a minute, Chuckie. Listen! The music stopped!" exclaimed Tommy. "Maybe the ghosts got scareded by our costumes and left. Let's look!"

"I wouldn't do that if I were you," warned Angelica.

"I'm not going to look," said Chuckie firmly.

"Me neither," said Phil.

"Me neither," said Lil.

"Well, maybe all of us . . . uh-oh," Tommy trailed off. A shadow fell over the babies.
A terrifying creature had sprung up from behind the couch and was standing over them.

Tommy gulped as the creature bent down to pick him up.

"Don't worry, Tommy!" said the creature. "It's just me, Daddy! How do you like my costume? Hey, Deed? Have you seen my vampire teeth anywhere?"

"Try the basement!" Didi called back. Stu put Tommy down and headed downstairs.

"You see, Chuckie? That was just my dad," said Tommy.
"Maybe the ghosts and gobblings aren't going to bother us!" said Phil.
"Maybe they all flew away because they heard your dad say this was the scarediest house on the block," added Lil.
Suddenly the lights flickered and went out.

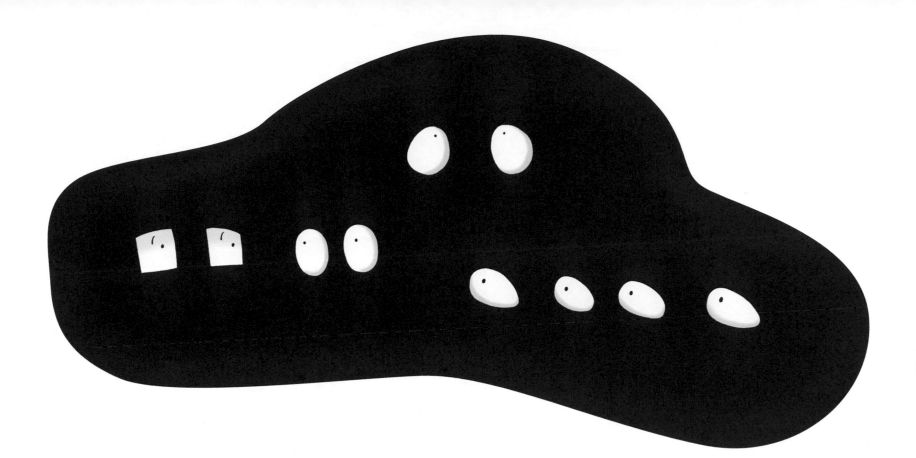

"What was that? A gobbling?" whimpered Chuckie.

"What *is* a gobbling, anyway?" asked Phil.

"I'm not sure," said Chuckie.

"Hey, this isn't funny! What happened to the lights?" Angelica yelled.
"Turn them back on!"

Stu called up from the basement. "Sorry, Deed! I guess my power drill
finally bit the dust! Must have blown a fuse. I'll find the fusebox!"

A moment later the lights flickered back on.

The babies blinked. Angelica looked relieved.

"That does it! Let's give Angelica our candy so she can give it to the ghosts and grumblins," said Chuckie. "Then maybe they'll get out of here for good."

"Maybe you're right, Chuckie," Tommy finally agreed.

One by one the babies began dumping their candy into Angelica's lap. But she wasn't paying attention. She was listening to a noise coming from upstairs.

Stomp! Stomp! Stomp!

"Okay, enough already!" yelled Angelica at the ceiling. "I was just trying to get a little extra candy!"

Suddenly Chuckie shrieked. "A grumblin! Look! It's coming down the stairs to get us!"

"Angelica, you said if we gave you all our candy you'd get all the scaredy ghosts to go away!" said Tommy. "Tell them to go away now, please!"

"I'm getting out of here!" cried Angelica. "Aunt Didi!" she yelled as she ran into the kitchen.

The babies watched the ghost untangle itself from the sheet. It was Grandpa Lou!

"Never could figure out how to fold these fitted sheets," he said to the babies. "But at least I found my teeth in the laundry basket."

Didi came out of the kitchen. "Angelica's a little overexcited," she said to Grandpa. "My wheat-germ muffins are almost ready! Come on, Pop. I'll put Dil to bed and help you fold the laundry. Then it's time to get my costume on!"

Angelica poked her head into the living room. "Is the grumblin gone?"
she asked shakily.

"Yes, Angelica, but you know who it was?" Tommy began. "It was just my . . ."

Wah-ha-ha-haaaaaaa!

An evil laugh came from the basement. Tommy, Chuckie, Phil, and Lil froze.
Angelica shrieked and ran back into the kitchen.

Stu came upstairs from the basement. He was carrying a box with a push button on it. "Check this out, kids!" he said. "I just rigged up a spooky Halloween doorbell!" He pressed the button, and the babies heard the same evil laugh. "The trick-or-treaters will love it!" He walked out to the front stoop to install it.

"You know what I think?" said Tommy to his friends. "I think the spirits of Halloween aren't here anymore! Let's go look behind the couch right now." He walked behind the couch and found the toy piano.

"See? It was just my toy piano making that music.
And these are just toys you wind up!"
Angelica crept cautiously out of the kitchen.

"Angelica, we want our candy back!" Tommy demanded. "The spirits aren't here. They must've gotten scareded away because our house is the scarediest one on the block."

"Who cares about candy at a time like this!" said Angelica. "I never thought real spirits were going to . . ."

Yeeeeee-oooooow! came a screech from outside. Everyone jumped.

"There really are spirits around here!" Angelica shrieked. "I better go get the candy I hid from you babies and give it to them." She ran from the room. Stu came rushing downstairs. "Is Spike after that neighbor's cat again?" he muttered to himself as he dashed outside to find the dog.

Angelica returned, lugging a big bucket of candy. Didi came downstairs in her Halloween costume.

"Come on, kids," said Didi. "I think my muffins are done. You can be the first to try them! My goodness, Angelica. You look as though you've seen a ghost!"

"I don't feel very well, Aunt Didi," moaned Angelica.

Didi felt her forehead, then settled her onto the sofa. "I'll be right back, honey," she said and led the babies toward the kitchen.

Spike scratched at the kitchen door, and Didi let him inside. Stu was right behind him. Didi passed out muffins to the babies. "I'm going to go check on Angelica," she said to Stu and hurried out.

Wah-ha-haaaa! the doorbell rang.

"Our first trick-or-treaters!" yelped Stu. He rushed out of the kitchen after Didi. As he left, his long cape knocked a container of flour off the counter.

"Maybe we should go tell Angelica that the scaredy guys are not here anymore?" said Tommy.

"She did look a little scareded," agreed Chuckie.

"Yeah, and maybe she'll give us our candy back," added Lil.

The babies, followed by Spike, ran out of the kitchen.

Angelica took one look at the babies and Spike and shrieked. "Go away, spirits!" she wailed. "Go away! I didn't mean to take all the candy! Here! Take it!" She began heaving Halloween candy out of the folds of her costume and flinging it toward the babies.

"How nice of you to share your candy, Angelica," said Didi as she walked into the room. "Stu, would you please clean the kids up? I'm taking Angelica upstairs to put her to bed. I think she's had a little too much sugar."

"Okay," said Stu. "I'll take the kids upstairs for bathtime. You know what, Deed? I think that's it for trick-or-treaters! For some reason, they seem to have gotten scared off! What are we going to do with all this candy?"

After bathtime Tommy fed Spike his wheat-germ muffin. Then the babies
all sat down next to the big bowl of Halloween candy.

"I wasn't really scareded at all tonight. Were you, Tommy?" asked Chuckie
between bites.

"Nope! I wasn't either," Tommy replied. "I guess the spirits of Halloween
aren't so scary after all!"